FIRST CAROLS

illustrated by

BRENDA MEREDITH SEYMOUR

The Lutterworth Press

Copyright © 1967 **The Lutterworth Press**

This impression 1991

Printed in Hong Kong by Colorcraft Ltd

The Publishers wish to make acknowledgement to the following for permission to include carols of which they control the copyright: Oxford University Press ("Little Jesus, sweetly sleep" and 'Unto us a Boy is born" from the *Oxford Book of Carols*); and Miss D. E. Collins ("How Far is it to Bethlehem?").

CONTENTS

THE FIRST NOWELL

The first Nowell the angel did say
Was to certain poor shepherds in fields
as they lay;
In fields where they lay a-keeping their
sheep
On a cold winter's night that was so
deep:

Nowell, Nowell, Nowell, Nowell,
Born is the King of Israel.

They lookèd up and saw a star,
Shining in the East, beyond them far,
And to the earth it gave great light,
And so it continued both day and night:

And by the light of that same star,
Three wise men came from country far;
To seek for a king was their intent,
And to follow the star wherever it went:

This star drew nigh to the North-West,
O'er Bethlehem it took its rest,
And there it did both stop and stay
Right over the place where Jesus lay:

Then entered in those wise men three,
Full reverently upon their knee,
And offered there in His presence
Their gold and myrrh and frankincense:

Then let us all with one accord
Sing praises to our heavenly Lord,
That hath made heaven and earth of
                                nought,
And with His blood mankind hath
                                bought:

HARK! THE HERALD ANGELS SING

Hark! the herald angels sing
Glory to the new-born King,
Peace on earth, and mercy mild,
God and sinners reconciled.
Joyful, all ye nations, rise,
Join the triumph of the skies;
With the angelic host proclaim:
'Christ is born in Bethlehem:'

Hark! the herald angels sing
Glory to the new-born King.

Christ, by highest heaven adored,
Christ, the everlasting Lord,
Late in time behold Him come,
Offspring of a virgin's womb!
Veiled in flesh the Godhead see;
Hail the incarnate Deity!
Pleased as man with men to dwell,
Jesus, our Immanuel:

Mild He lays His glory by,
Born that man no more may die,
Born to raise the sons of earth,
Born to give them second birth.
Hail the heaven-born Prince of Peace!
Hail the Sun of Righteousness!
Light and life to all He brings,
Risen with healing in His wings.

Charles Wesley

IT CAME UPON THE MIDNIGHT CLEAR

It came upon the midnight clear,
   That glorious song of old,
From angels bending near the earth
   To touch their harps of gold:
'Peace on the earth, good-will to men,
   From heaven's all-gracious King!'
The world in solemn stillness lay
   To hear the angels sing.

Still through the cloven skies they come
   With peaceful wings unfurled;
And still their heavenly music floats
   O'er all the weary world;
Above its sad and lowly plains
   They bend on hovering wing,
And ever o'er its Babel-sounds
   The blessèd angels sing.

But with the woes of sin and strife
  The world has suffered long;
Beneath the angel strain have rolled
  Two thousand years of wrong;
And man, at war with man, hears not
  The love song which they bring.
O hush the noise, ye men of strife,
  And hear the angels sing.

For lo! the days are hastening on,
  By prophet bards foretold,
When with the ever-circling years
  Comes round the age of gold,
When peace shall over all the earth
  Its ancient splendours fling,
And the whole world give back the song
  Which now the angels sing.

Edmund Hamilton Sears

WHILE SHEPHERDS WATCHED

While shepherds watched their flocks by
                                    night,
  All seated on the ground,
The angel of the Lord came down,
  And glory shone around.

'Fear not!' said he; for mighty dread
    Had seized their troubled mind;
'Glad tidings of great joy I bring
    To you and all mankind.

'To you, in David's town, this day
    Is born, of David's line,
A Saviour, who is Christ the Lord;
    And this shall be the sign:

'The heavenly Babe you there shall find
    To human view displayed,
All meanly wrapped in swathing bands,
    And in a manger laid.'

Thus spake the seraph; and forthwith
   Appeared a shining throng
Of angels praising God, and thus
   Addressed their joyful song:

'All Glory be to God on high,
   And to the earth be peace;
Good will henceforth from heaven to
                   men

   Begin and never cease!'

Nahum Tate

HOW FAR IS IT TO BETHLEHEM?

How far is it to Bethlehem?
    Not very far.
Shall we find the stable-room,
    Lit by a star?

Can we see the little Child,
    Is he within?
If we lift the wooden latch
    May we go in?

May we stroke the creatures there,
    Ox, ass or sheep?
May we peep like them and see
    Jesus asleep?

If we touch His tiny hand
    Will He awake?
Will he know we've come so far
    Just for His sake?

Frances Chesterton

O LITTLE TOWN OF BETHLEHEM

O little town of Bethlehem,
  How still we see thee lie!
Above thy deep and dreamless sleep
  The silent stars go by.
Yet in thy dark street shineth
  The everlasting Light;
The hopes and fears of all the years
  Are met in thee to-night.

O morning stars, together
  Proclaim the holy birth,
And praises sing to God the King,
  And peace to men on earth.
For Christ is born of Mary;
  And, gathered all above,
While mortals sleep, the angels keep
  Their watch of wondering love.

How silently, how silently
  The wondrous gift is given!
So God imparts to human hearts
  The blessings of His heaven.
No ear may hear His coming;
  But in this world of sin,
Where meek souls will receive Him, still
  The dear Christ enters in.

O holy Child of Bethlehem,
  Descend to us, we pray;
Cast out our sin, and enter in;
  Be born in us to-day.
We hear the Christmas angels
  The great glad tidings tell;
O come to us, abide with us,
  Our Lord Immanuel.

Phillips Brooks

WE THREE KINGS OF ORIENT ARE

We three kings of Orient are;
Bearing gifts we traverse afar
Field and fountain, moor and mountain,
Following yonder star:

   O star of wonder, star of night,
   Star with royal beauty bright,
   Westward leading, still proceeding,
   Guide us to Thy perfect light!

Melchior
Born a king on Bethlehem plain,
Gold I bring, to crown him again—
King for ever, ceasing never,
Over us all to reign:

Gaspar
Frankincense to offer have I;
Incense owns a Deity nigh;
Prayer and praising all men raising,
Worship him, God most high:

Balthazar

Myrrh is mine; its bitter perfume
Breathes a life of gathering gloom;
Sorrowing, sighing, bleeding, dying,
Sealed in the stone-cold tomb:

Glorious now, behold Him arise,
King, and God, and sacrifice!
Heaven sings 'Alleluia',
'Alleluia' the earth replies:

John Henry Hopkins

ONCE IN ROYAL DAVID'S CITY

Once in royal David's city
　　Stood a lowly cattle-shed,
Where a mother laid her baby
　　In a manger for His bed.
Mary was that mother mild,
Jesus Christ her little child.

He came down to earth from heaven
    Who is God and Lord of all,
And His shelter was a stable,
    And His cradle was a stall.
With the poor, and mean, and lowly,
Lived on earth our Saviour holy.

And through all His wondrous childhood
    He would honour and obey,
Love and watch the lowly maiden
    In whose gentle arms He lay.
Christian children all must be
Mild, obedient, good as He.

For He is our childhood's pattern:
  Day by day like us He grew;
He was little, weak and helpless;
  Tears and smiles like us He knew;
And He feeleth for our sadness,
And He shareth in our gladness.

And our eyes at last shall see Him,
  Through His own redeeming love;
For that Child so dear and gentle
  Is our Lord in heaven above;
And He leads His children on
To the place where He is gone.

Cecil Frances Alexander

As with Gladness

As with gladness men of old
Did the guiding star behold,
As with joy they hailed its light,
Leading onward, beaming bright;
So, most gracious Lord, may we
Evermore be led to Thee.

As with joyful steps they sped,
Saviour, to Thy lowly bed,
There to bend the knee before
Thee, whom heaven and earth adore;
So may we with willing feet,
Ever seek the mercy-seat.

As they offered gifts most rare
At Thy cradle rude and bare;
So may we with holy joy,
Pure, and free from sin's alloy,
All our costliest treasures bring,
Christ, to Thee, our heavenly King.

Holy Jesus, every day
Keep us in the narrow way;
And, when earthly things are past,
Bring our ransomed souls at last
Where they need no star to guide,
Where no clouds Thy glory hide.

In the heavenly country bright
Need they no created light;
Thou its light, its joy, its crown,
Thou its sun which goes not down;
There for ever may we sing
Hallelujahs to our King.

William Chatterton Dix

O COME, ALL YE FAITHFUL

O come, all ye faithful,
    Joyful and triumphant;
Come ye, O come ye to Bethlehem;
    Come and behold Him
    Born the King of angels:
O come, let us adore Him, Christ the
                  Lord.

    True God of true God,
    Light of Light eternal,
Lo! He abhors not the Virgin's womb,
    Son of the Father,
    Begotten, not created:
O come, let us adore Him, Christ the
                  Lord.

Sing, choirs of angels,
Sing in exultation,
Sing, all ye citizens of heaven above,
Sing ye, 'All glory
To God in the highest!'
O come, let us adore Him, Christ the
Lord.

Yea, Lord, we greet Thee,
Born this happy morning;
Jesus, to Thee be glory given,
Word of the Father,
Now in flesh appearing:
O come, let us adore Him, Christ the
Lord.

UNTO US A BOY IS BORN

Unto us a boy is born,
    King of all creation!
Came He to a world forlorn,
    The Lord of every nation.

Cradled in a stall was He,
    With sleepy cows and asses;
But the very beasts could see
    That He all men surpasses.

Herod then with fear was filled:
    'A Prince,' he said, 'in Jewry!'
All the little boys he killed
    At Bethlehem in his fury.

Now may Mary's son, who came
  So long ago to love us,
Lead us all with hearts aflame
  Unto the joys above us.

Omega and Alpha He!
  Let the organ thunder,
While the choir with peals of glee
  Doth rend the air asunder.

LITTLE JESUS, SWEETLY SLEEP

Little Jesus, sweetly sleep, do not stir;
We will lend a coat of fur,
   We will rock you, rock you, rock you,
   We will rock you, rock you, rock
                     you;
See the fur to keep you warm
Snugly round your tiny form.

Mary's little baby, sleep, sweetly sleep,
Sleep in comfort, slumber deep;
  We will rock you, rock you, rock you,
  We will rock you, rock you, rock
                                    you;

We will serve you all we can,
Darling, darling little man.

THE HOLLY AND THE IVY

The holly and the ivy,
When they are both full grown,
Of all the trees that are in the wood,
The holly bears the crown:

The rising of the sun,
And the running of the deer,
The playing of the merry organ,
Sweet singing in the choir.

The holly bears a blossom,
As white as the lily flower,
And Mary bore sweet Jesus Christ
To be our sweet Saviour:

The holly bears a berry,
As red as any blood,
And Mary bore sweet Jesus Christ
To do poor sinners good:

The holly bears a prickle,
As sharp as any thorn,
And Mary bore sweet Jesus Christ
On Christmas Day in the morn:

The holly bears a bark,
As bitter as any gall,
And Mary bore sweet Jesus Christ
For to redeem us all:

The holly and the ivy,
When they are both full grown,
Of all the trees that are in the wood,
The holly bears the crown.

I SAW THREE SHIPS

I saw three ships come sailing in,
On Christmas Day, on Christmas Day,
I saw three ships come sailing in,
On Christmas Day in the morning.

And what was in those ships all three?
Our Saviour Christ and his lady.

Pray, whither sailed those ships all three?
O, they sailed into Bethlehem.

And all the bells on earth shall ring,
And all the angels in Heaven shall sing,

And all the souls on earth shall sing.
Then let us all rejoice amain!

LOVE CAME DOWN AT CHRISTMAS

Love came down at Christmas,
  Love all lovely, Love Divine,
Love was born at Christmas,
  Star and angels gave the sign.

Worship we the Godhead,
  Love Incarnate, Love Divine,
Worship we our Jesus:
  But wherewith for sacred sign?

Love shall be our token,
  Love be yours and love be mine,
Love to God and all men
  Love for plea and gift and sign.

Christina Rossetti